MERMICORN ISLAND #2

Narwhal Adventure!

BY JASON JUNE

Scholastic Inc.

To Tayrra, Caytlyn, and Brennon! Dream so big that you'll never need a Grow Shell!

Copyright © 2021 by Jason June

Cover and interior art copyright © 2021 by Lisa Manuzak Wiley

All rights reserved. Published by Scholastic Inc., *Publishers since 1920*. SCHOLASTIC and associated logos are trademarks and/or registered trademarks of Scholastic Inc.

The publisher does not have any control over and does not assume any responsibility for author or third-party websites or their content.

No part of this publication may be reproduced, stored in a retrieval system, or transmitted in any form or by any means, electronic, mechanical, photocopying, recording, or otherwise, without written permission of the publisher. For information regarding permission, write to Scholastic Inc., Attention: Permissions Department, 557 Broadway, New York, NY 10012.

This book is a work of fiction. Names, characters, places, and incidents are either the product of the author's imagination or are used fictitiously, and any resemblance to actual persons, living or dead, business establishments, events, or locales is entirely coincidental.

ISBN 978-1-338-68519-0

10 9 8 7 6 5 4 3 2 1   21 22 23 24 25

Printed in the U.S.A. 40

First printing 2021

Book design by Yaffa Jaskoll

MEET NELIA NARWHAL

"**Oh my goldfish**, Ruby, this cake is **mer-mazing**!" I said, starting in on my second slice of sea sponge cake. It was vanilla-y and covered in frosting with barnacle berries on top.

"And so are these angelfish food cake doughnuts," Flash agreed. "And those crab cutout cookies, and these

sea-salted caramel tarts! All of it is
fin-credible!"

Flash always talked a million miles a
minute, but with his mouth full, about
a million crumbs flew everywhere.

Echo's dorsal fin shook with
excitement. "You are for sure going to

win the Beluga Bakery Sugar Castle Competition tomorrow."

The Sugar Castle Competition was the most **sea-licious** Mermicorn Island tradition. Every year, **any-fishy** who loved to make desserts could enter their own sandcastle made out of sweet baked treats. Ruby's magic— her BAKING SPARKLE—was perfect for making Sugar Castles.

All sea creatures in Mermicorn Island have powers. We call it having SPARKLE. Echo and all the other dolphins have magic echolocation that helps them find things. Flash and all the other seahorses have magical superspeed. Mermicorns each get their own unique SPARKLE, and Ruby's lets her make baked goods.

My SPARKLE hasn't come in yet, but I was still able to help with the competition. Ruby knows how much I love to draw, so she let me design the Sugar Castle.

"I've been working my tail off to get all these pastries and cakes just right," Ruby said.

Ruby squinted her eyes and wiggled her tail. She always did that before she was about to do magic. Red sparkles flew from Ruby's horn and turned into a perfectly round, perfectly golden sea-salted caramel tart.

"You really have been working so hard, Ruby," I said. "Remember when you could only make cupcakes with your magic?"

"*Mmm*, cupcakes," Flash said. "Maybe you should make some more of those. I could always eat another cupcake. I love your cupcakes." Flash was always hungry. He needed a lot of energy for his magical seahorse superspeed.

Ruby blushed. Her cheeks matched the color of her red tail. "Thanks! And now I can make pies, breads, cakes, cookies, and tarts like this one."

She added the tart to the pile
of desserts she'd stacked onto her
captain's-wheel kitchen table. Ruby's
house was made out of an old sunken
ship! We put on plays for our parents
on the roof deck sometimes, with a
spotlight following us from the crow's
nest.

"Just having tasty treats isn't going to be enough to make my Sugar Castle stand out," Ruby said. "All the entries in the Sugar Castle Competition are going to be **sea-licious**. The castle needs to look **fin-tastic** too. Luckily, Lucky has that covered!"

I pulled out my Sugar Castle drawing. On it was a picture of a kraken, my favorite magical creature. Krakens look like massive giant squids but hadn't been seen in Mermicorn Island for hundreds of years.

"Our Sugar Castle is going to look like a kraken," I said, showing Flash and

Echo my drawing. "The tentacles will be the turrets. Doughnuts are the tentacle suckers. And sea-salted caramel tarts are the eyes!"

"**Mermidude**," Flash said. "**No-fishy** out there will think of something this great. It's the best Sugar Castle design ever!"

Echo nodded. "Yep, you two are totally going to win."

"Lucky's design is the best, isn't it?" Ruby said. "But when I tried to make my cakes turn into tentacles, I couldn't get them to look right. They kept coming out more like the electric eel cupcakes I made for Flash's birthday."

My tail drooped. "Oh, **blobfish**,"
I said. "But if **any-fishy** can think of
a **fin-tastic** idea to make tentacles,
it's the **Fin-tastic Four**."

The **Fin-tastic Four** was the
name we used for our group of four
BFFFs: best fin friends forever. It was
me, Ruby, Flash, and Echo, together for
every adventure.

An idea swam into my head. "Maybe
there's a magic shell from Poseidon's
chest that can help us make **mer-
mazing** shapes."

Poseidon is the most magical

mermicorn in all the seven seas. He can use every type of SPARKLE known to **mer-kind**. Poseidon even gave me a whole treasure chest full of magic shells a few weeks ago after Ruby and I escaped a bunch of hungry electric eels. I may not have SPARKLE of my own yet, but the shells give me special powers, just as if I had my own magic. My friends and I call it SHELL SPARKLE. So far we'd found a shell that turned me invisible, one that let me grow seaweed, and another that let me speak Dogfish.

"Actually, I found **some-fishy** who can help," Ruby said. "My pen pal, Nelia, came in from Atlantis to visit her aunt and uncle, and she's got SPARKLE that would be perfect for the job." A knock came from a porthole window. "That must be her!"

Ruby swam to the porthole and pushed it open. The first thing that came through was a shiny, spiral horn. I thought it would be another mermicorn. But then the horn kept going and going and going. It was the longest unicorn horn I'd ever seen!

Then, finally, the fishy attached to the horn swam inside. It wasn't a mermicorn at all. It was a narwhal!

"**EVERY-fishy**, meet my friend, Nelia," Ruby said. "Her TWISTY-TURNY SPARKLE is going to get us first place in the Sugar Castle Competition!"

TWISTY-TURNY TREATS

"Nice to meet you, Nelia!" I said. "I've never seen TWISTY-TURNY SPARKLE in real life before. I'm excited to see it in action."

"I heard that TWISTY-TURNY SPARKLE is how the best rides at the Narwhal Adventure Theme Park were made," Echo said.

Just like all other creatures in Mermicorn Island, narwhals have a magic power. With their superlong and spiral-shaped horns, narwhals are able to make everything twist and turn into the most **mer-mazing** shapes. Narwhals made Twisty-Turny Taffy, one of my favorite candies, which comes in loop the loops! And they made the **fin-credible** spiral bookshelves in the new Sea Glass Library.

"My aunt and uncle own the theme park!" Nelia said. "I'm actually in Mermicorn Island visiting them. We should all go sometime!"

"That would be **fin-tastic**," I said. "**Wait a minnow.** Are we going to use your magic to turn our Sugar Castle into a big baked ride?"

"Hold your seahorses!" Flash said. "That's the best idea ever! With sugar slides and roller coaster cookies."

Nelia threw her head back and laughed. Her horn was so long, it hit the ceiling!

"That would be fun," Nelia said when she stopped giggling. "My SPARKLE isn't strong enough to make a whole baked theme park. But it can do this."

Nelia floated toward the captain's-wheel table. She dipped her horn so that it gently touched a sea sponge cake. Then she hummed softly, and a bright yellow light flowed down her horn. When the light hit the cake, the sea sponge twisted and curved and turned itself into a kraken tentacle.

"No way," I said. "Your magic is **mer-mazing**, Nelia. And your horn is **sea-utiful**."

"Thanks," Nelia said. "My horn is actually a tusk. That's a type of tooth. All narwhals have a magical tooth that grows from their forehead."

Flash flashed a big toothy grin. "I wish all my teeth were magical!"

Nelia laughed and tapped her tusk against each baked treat on the table. With every tap, the dough moved and stacked. Nelia was building the Sugar Castle before our eyes!

Sea sponge cake twisted and turned.

Sea-salted caramel tarts curved and oozed into golden eye shapes. Angelfish food cake doughnuts wriggled and bent. All the baked goods became the twistiest, turniest kraken-shaped Sugar Castle I had ever seen!

As a finishing touch, Ruby used her

Baking Sparkle to make crab cutout cookies for castle guards.

Echo looked at the Sugar Castle, her eyes so big that barnacle berries reflected in them. "Nelia, it's perfect," she said. "There's no way you three can be beat!"

"That's what I'm hoping," Nelia said.

Ruby stared at the kraken Sugar Castle. There were really deep wrinkles in her forehead. Deeper-than-the-Sea-Dragon-Trench deep.

"What's wrong, Ruby?" I asked.

Ruby sighed and crossed her hooves. "I love our Sugar Castle. You, me, and Nelia make a great team. But I went to the Beluga Bakery Competition last year, and the castles were huge. Ours fits easily on the kitchen table. There's no way a castle this small will win."

Winning the Sugar Castle Competition was a big deal for Ruby. The winner got to study under Baxter Beluga, the best baker in town. When she grew up, Ruby dreamed of opening a dessert theater, where customers got to eat her delicious baked goods while she performed plays. She wanted to bake the best recipes with Baxter to really make her dessert theater stand out.

"*Hmmm*, you're right," Flash agreed. "I remember going last year too. The castles were so big, I bet eating one of them would actually make me full."

"Then those castles must be huge," I said. "Can your TWISTY-TURNY SPARKLE make things stretch bigger, Nelia?"

She shook her head. Her long tusk accidentally brushed through my mane as she moved her head from side to side.

"Unfortunately, no," Nelia said.
"I can make anything twisty-turny, but
I can't grow things bigger than their
normal size. Do any of you have GR⊛W
SParkle?"

Echo didn't shake her head, but her

dorsal fin sure shook. "No, but we might

have GROW Shell Sparkle!"

"What's that?" Nelia asked.

I swam to Ruby's porthole door

and waved for the group to follow me.

"Come on! I'll show you!"

MASSIVE MANE EVENT

Poseidon's treasure chest was where I always left it: right at the foot of my bed. The chest filled my bedroom with a golden glow. My favorite Leonardo da Fishy poster looked **mer-mazing** in the glittery light!

I flipped open the lid. Dozens of sparkly seashells lay in front of us.

"There are so many," Nelia said. "How will we know which one has GROW SPARKLE?"

"I always just reach for the shell that feels right," I said.

That's how I found the DOGFISH SPARKLE SHELL. Flash wanted to have a sleepover at his house. But Floofy, his dogfish, has magical barks that make us fall asleep before we get to have any fun. I looked for a shell that could solve the problem, and felt a pull in my hooves toward the one that let me speak Dogfish. That's how I learned Floofy barked all the time because he gets gassy. Now he eats kelp kibble and doesn't fart or bark at all!

"Pick that one!" Flash pointed toward a big black shell with white stripes. "No, that one!" This time he pointed at one that was purple and yellow. "Oh, wait, that's the one! I know it!" Now he was looking at a shell with green stars all over it.

But the pull in my hooves told me the shell I needed was different. It was an orange conch shell that was bigger than all the rest.

"I think that's the one," I said, and pointed to the conch.

"Ooooh. Grab it, Lucky, and let's get this adventure started!" Echo said. "I can't wait to see what happens."

"And I'll grab the trident," Flash said. "I'll be right back in—wait for it—a flash!" He laughed and clapped his fins together.

With a burst of magical superspeed, Flash sped out my window and back in two seconds. He held his shiny toy trident. "Here you go. Put the conch shell in, and let's see what happens."

Poseidon controls all the SPaRKle in the sea with his trident. When he left me his treasure chest full of magic shells, he said Flash's toy trident could help me control each shell's power.

I took the conch in my hooves. The most **mer-mazing** feeling of warm, tingly bubbles flowed from my tail to my horn. Magic! I placed the conch right below the three prongs of Flash's trident. It stuck snugly, like there was a magical magnet meant just for shells.

"What now?" Nelia asked. "How does it work?"

"I usually just wave the trident and picture what I want to happen," I said.

"But we left the Sugar Castle back at Ruby's house." Echo groaned. "How will we know if this is the GR⊛W Shell?"

"Oh, I know!" Ruby said. She ran a hoof through her mane. "I want to grow my mane out for the role of Rapunzel at the Mermicorn Island Theater. Try the GR⊛W Shell SParKle on my mane!"

"Okay," I said. "Hold very still." I thought super hard. My tongue poked out between my teeth. I pictured Ruby's mane growing twice as long.

"Hair we go," I whispered, and waved the trident.

The warm bubbly tingles of magic went from my hoof all the way down to the tip of my tail. Then big orange bubbles billowed out of the opening in the conch shell. They floated toward Ruby. They popped all around her mane, and her bright red hair started to grow!

"It's working!" Echo said.

"And it tickles!" Ruby giggled. By the

time her mane stopped growing, it was halfway down her tail.

"Look at all that hair," Flash said. "That's the most epic mane I've ever seen on a mermicorn in my whole life!"

Ruby looked at herself in my bedroom mirror. "This is perfect, Lucky! I will definitely get that Rapunzel part."

"I might be able to help," Nelia said. She hummed her TWiStY-TURnY tune. When her tusk glowed yellow, she tapped it against Ruby's mane. All Ruby's hair curled up into the most **mer-nificent** hairdo.

"Wow, Nelia," Ruby said. "You could open your own hair salon."

Nelia smiled. "Thanks, but I'm thinking 'Beluga Bakery Sugar Castle co-champion' has a nice ring to it. With your BAKING SPARKLE, my TWISTY-TURNY MAGIC, and Lucky's GROW SHELL, there's no way we are going to lose tomorrow!"

CRACKS IN THE
COMPETITION

The next day, our parents dropped us
off in Mermicorn Island Square. Dad
made **BUBBLES** that spelled **GOOD
LUCK**, then swam off to go shopping
while we got our Sugar Castle set up.

The square was *packed* with every
type of sea creature you could imagine:

The Turtlebergs sold Sugar Castle Competition T-shirts at their clothing store, Express Your Shell; the mermaid band Mer-made for Music sang near the bubble fountain; and Sadie the octopus painted eight mermicorns' faces at once.

But the most noticeable thing of all was three **fin-credible** Sugar Castles outside the Beluga Bakery.

"Holy mackerel!" Flash said. "Look at that Sugar Castle over there. It's covered in sea dragon ice frosting! I bet if you licked it, your tongue would get stuck!"

Echo pointed to the one next to it.
"And that one is made by selkies with
cookie dough guards that change shape!
Look, they're sharks. Now they're squids.
Now they're sea cucumbers!"

"That one says it's covered with

starfish that can grant wishes," Nelia said, pointing with her long tusk. "How in the ocean did they find real-life Wish upon a Starfish? They're so rare!"

If it was any other year, we would all flip tail over horn for the Sugar Castles. But this year, the castles were our competition.

The giggle that was usually in Nelia's voice was nowhere to be found. "Our castle is just Twisty-Turny," she said. "There's no way we're going to win." Her tail drooped to the ocean floor.

"Plus, all those castles are huge," Ruby added. "More than three times as big as ours. You could fit inside them. Some of them would make a really good set for a play, actually."

Normally, talk of putting on plays made Ruby happy. But she looked really bummed out.

Baxter Beluga, owner of the Beluga Bakery, swam through the sea dragons' Sugar Castle with a crab claw clipboard in his flippers. He shivered when he swam by the ice frosting. Even from across the square, I could see him give the sea dragons five gold starfish on his judging sheet.

"Do you think the GR⊛W Shell

could make our castle that big?" Nelia
asked.

I opened my backpack and pulled out
Flash's toy trident. The orange GROW
Shell was attached. My whole body
tingled with that warm magic feeling.
It gave me so much hope. I just knew
we could still win the Sugar Castle
Competition.

"You bet your bottom sand dollar
it can make our castle that big," I said.
"It can make ours the biggest Sugar
Castle that's ever been seen!"

I waved the trident back and forth
and thought, *Make our Sugar Castle*

HUGE! Then I pictured the castle growing and growing and growing. I thought about the sea sponge cake tentacles and the sea-salted caramel tarts and the angelfish doughnuts getting super big.

Glowing orange **BUBBLES** poured out of the GR⭐W Shell's opening and streamed toward our Sugar Castle. Each **BUBBLE** popped against the twisty baked goods. The sugary treats grew two times bigger. Then three times!

"You're doing it, **mermidude**," Flash said. "This is going to be so big, we can all move in! We'll each have our own room! Ooh, be sure it's big enough that I can have a racetrack. And a closet for all my racing goggles!"

The magic **BUBBLES** popped against our Sugar Castle until it was as big as the others in the square.

"That's perfect, Lucky," Ruby said. "I think that should do it."

"Sounds great," I said.

Our castle was big enough now that other fishies noticed. Before I could picture the magic stopping, our friend from school Roger the jellyfish drifted over.

"**Oh my goldfish**, your Sugar Castle is ginormous!" Roger said. "I bet my uncle Leon could even fit in there. His tentacles are over a hundred feet long!"

Speaking of tentacles, Roger wasn't very good at keeping track of his. He was so distracted by our Sugar Castle that he didn't see where they were going. One of them drifted right into Nelia, stinging her.

"Yowch!" she yelped. She jumped out of Roger's reach. Her tusk swung toward our castle and straight into the stream of magic GR⊛W Shell bubbles! Then her tusk knocked the trident right from my hooves. It crashed against the square's oyster cobblestones.

I rushed to pick up the trident. When I had it in my hooves, the tingly magic feeling left my body.

The GR⊛W Shell was broken.

5

GROWING AND GROWING
AND GROWING

"Oh, **blobfish**," I moaned. I'd never broken one of Poseidon's magic shells before.

"Whoops!" Roger said. "It's always hard to keep track of these tentacles. Are you all right, Nelia?"

"Yes, but it doesn't look like that

shell is." Nelia rushed forward, extra careful of where her tusk went this time. "I'm so sorry, Lucky. Can we fix it?"

There was a huge crack in the front of the shell. I tried to take it off the trident, but it was stuck. The shell glowed a dull orange instead of bright orange. It looked like it was sick.

"This has never happened before," I said. "I don't know how to fix it."

"Um, **e-e-every-fishy**?" Ruby stuttered. She shook so much the curls in her new hairdo bounced up and down.

"I think we've got bigger problems than the broken shell."

"Yeah." Flash nodded at superspeed. "Really big. Really, really, really, really BIG!"

I turned around to see what they were looking at.

Our Sugar Castle was humongous! And with a funny **BLOOP** sound, it grew bigger right before our eyes!

The sea sponge cake tentacles stood taller than the Beluga Bakery. The crab cutout cookies loomed over me. I had to flick my tail to float out of the way before I got knocked over by an angelfish food cake doughnut.

Nelia turned to me. "How do we get it to–"

BLOOP!

"Ow!" I yelped.

Nelia's tusk poked me in the eye. But not because she wasn't looking where

she was going. Nelia and her tusk were growing too!

"Does your tusk normally grow like that?" Ruby asked.

Nelia shook her head. "This is totally not narwhal normal."

BLOOP!

Our Sugar Castle kept moving. One of the crab cutout cookie claws burst forward with magical growth and knocked into Echo. She flipped tail over dorsal fin.

"Okay," Echo said when she finally stopped flipping. "I know I said I like adventure, but I've had enough for one day."

"I got it," I said. I squinted my eyes shut. It helped my stinging eye and let me picture everything and **every-fishy** completely still, no growing at all. Then I waved the trident twice.

I peeked my eyes open to see two icky orange **BUBBLES** flow from the broken GR☻W Shell. They popped against the sea dragon and Wish upon a Starfish Sugar Castles.

BLOOP!

Those castles started growing too. Waving the trident had made things worse!

"What's going on?" Baxter Beluga shouted. When he saw the panic on Nelia's face as she grew again, he dove right into help mode.

"Kids, are you all right?" He swam over, but—**BLOOP!**—our Sugar Castle doubled in size. Baxter had to dive out of the way so he wouldn't get stuck in giant caramel tart gooeyness.

"Not good, **mermidude**," Flash said. It was the shortest sentence I'd ever heard him say. That meant things were definitely not good.

And then they got worse.

CRASH!

6

MAKE A MAGICAL MESS

Our growing Sugar Castle knocked the selkie shape-shifting castle right over. Dough guards in the shape of seals, then lobsters, then anchovies flew everywhere. Puffs of powdered sugar covered everything. **Every-fishy** swam around waving their fins in a frenzy.

"What do we do?" I asked.

Baxter Beluga shrugged his flippers. "I don't think I can bake us out of this, kids. My TASTE SPARKLE can only turn sweet things savory, and savory things sweet. It can't stop runaway sea sponge cake."

BLOOP!

Nelia grew again. Her tusk jammed through the shell in the Express Your Shell sign. She was as big as a building now!

Nelia wiggled back and forth. "I'm stuck!"

The GROW Shell was still glowing that icky orange color. It was like it had turned sour. Maybe the magic in it had gone bad when the shell broke.

BLOOP!

Nelia grew once more and knocked the entire store over. "**oh my goldfish**. This is *definitely* not narwhal normal," she said.

Nelia swam over the square. Her

gigantic body cast a shadow over us.

"I'm getting too big!" she said. "If I stay in the square, I might break more things."

BLOOP!

I didn't have time to tell her everything would be okay because the sea dragon Sugar Castle grew again too. It swiped through the stage in the middle of the square. The mermaids of Mer-made for Music had to swim away so they weren't hit by frozen sea bass guitars.

I saw all our parents on the other side of the stage. It looked like they were trying to get to us, but there was so much growing that they couldn't get through. Flash's mom stretched her tail out just like Flash does before he's about to use his magical superspeed.

"I'm coming, kids!" Flash's mom said. She had a Speedy Seahorse Taxi saddle on her back. "I'll get you out of the square!"

BLOOP!

But the Sugar Castles were growing so big that they blocked Mrs. Finnegan before she could get to us.

"**Some-fishy** help!" Baxter hollered. "We've got runaway Sugar Castles!"

Two sea dragons dodged a giant doughnut. "We'll stop the castles with ice!" one of them said.

They swam close to our colossal Sugar Castle. Then they took three big breaths and blew magical ice all over our big baked kraken.

In seconds, the Sugar Castle was covered in frost. It looked like a gigantic ice sculpture. And the castle didn't budge at all.

"It worked!" Ruby cheered. "Thank you so–"

BLOOP!

Crack! Crick! Crack!

Lines popped all over the frozen castle.

BLOOP!

Ice burst everywhere, and our Sugar Castle grew even bigger! A sea sponge cake tentacle knocked over the **BUBBLE** fountain and swiped right toward us. Flash and I dove to the right. The toy trident and broken GR⊛W

Shell flew from my hooves. Echo and Ruby dove to the left.

SMASH!

The cake tentacle slammed down. **NO-fishy** was hurt, but now Flash and I were separated from our friends.

THINGS GET STICKY

Before I could think of a plan to get back to Ruby and Echo, two selkies swam over our heads.

"Don't worry, kids. We're going to use our Shape-Shifting Sparkle," one of them said. "We'll try to turn this castle into something soft that does less damage."

The two selkies wiggled their whiskers, and green glitter flowed from their noses. When the glitter touched a baked turret tentacle, it turned to jelly!

"Jelly is my jam!" Flash said. He slurped up some of the sugary goop with a big grin on his face. "This is the

most **sea-licious** selkie solution. Can I bottle some of this and take it home?"

The selkies moved to a tentacle that formed one of our Sugar Castle walls. With another whisker wiggle, that wall turned to jelly too.

"**Thank goldfish**," I said. "Everything is fixed."

But then—

BLOOP!

The jelly *and* all the Sugar Castles grew bigger. The jelly became so thick, Flash got trapped in it. He tugged and tugged his tail to try to get out. But it didn't work. Then he tried a burst of superspeed. That didn't work either.

"Lucky, I'm stuck!" Flash said. "My magic isn't working with my tail caught in all this jelly. What are we going to do?"

BLOOP!

Our Sugar Castle and all the jelly got bigger again. I couldn't see the selkies anywhere to ask for help.

"Lucky! Hurry!" Flash cried. "Get me out of here!"

Flash was now covered all the way to his neck. I had to tug him free or the jam would swallow him up!

I reached under the jelly and grabbed

Flash's fins. Then I pulled with all my might.

"Come on! Come on!" I said. I pictured Flash pulling free from the jelly. But unlike when I had a non-broken magic shell, thinking about what I wanted to happen didn't work. Flash was still stuck.

If only I had a SUPERSTRENGTH SPARKLE SHELL. I could try swimming home to look in Poseidon's treasure chest for one. But there was no way I would make it back in time. Flash would be swallowed up by the jam. And Mermicorn Island Square would be toppled over by gigantic baked goods.

I tugged and pulled and hoped, but it was no use. I needed more strength. Nelia definitely had strength now that she was huge. But she was so big there was no way she'd be able to help without smashing even more buildings.

I needed more fins or flippers to help me pull Flash out. I needed...

"**The Fin-Tastic Four**!" I shouted.

"Lucky!" Through all the baked goods, Echo's shout sounded like a whisper. "Where are you?"

I looked around, but I couldn't see Echo and Ruby anywhere. All I saw were

cake walls and giant cookies that grew
bigger by the minute.

"Nelia, can you see them?" I shouted
up at her.

She shook her head from above the
square. "The Sugar Castles are growing
too fast to see anything."

I knew of only one thing that could
help my friends find me.

"Echo!" I called. "Use your magic!"

I could just barely hear a few
musical clicks. It was Echo's magical
echolocation. She could find whatever
she was looking for with it, as long as it
wasn't too far away.

"Found you!" Echo yelled. "We'll be right there."

I looked up and saw Ruby and Echo way up high, swimming over a massive twisty-turny sea sponge cake tentacle.

BLOOP!

Everything got bigger again: Nelia, the Sugar Castles, and the jelly Flash was stuck in. It oozed so much that it covered his head. His whole body was stuck under the jelly.

"Hurry!" I yelled. "We've got to save Flash!"

"Don't worry!" Ruby called. "We're almost there!"

They were so close. They had made it over the last kraken castle tentacle and were almost to us.

BLOOP!

But then another growth burst happened, and a massive doughnut

sucker tumbled off a tentacle. It was the size of a boulder.

And it was going to fall right on top of my friends.

SMASHED TO PIECES

"Look out!" I screamed. My mane itched like it always does whenever I'm really, really nervous.

But at the same time I yelled, Echo shouted, "Almost there!" She didn't hear me.

I looked down into the jelly. Flash was looking up at me with wide, scared eyes.

"I promise I'll be right back," I said. "I'll be back in a…a flash."

Even with jelly all over him, I could still see him smile a bit. And that's what I needed. I needed to be like Flash. I thought all the fast thoughts I could muster, then swam toward Ruby and Echo with all my might.

My tail swished back and forth faster than it ever had before. I had to get to Ruby and Echo before they were squashed. I may not have had magical superspeed, but I was still pretty fast.

But so was the huge doughnut about to smoosh my friends.

"Lucky, slow down!" Ruby said.

I was just inches away from them.

"Yeah," Echo agreed. "You're going to run into us! *Oof!*"

I smacked right into her and Ruby. We tumbled manes over tails over flippers over horns. But we were safe.

CRASH!

The doughnut boulder smashed just an anchovy's length away.

Ruby looked at the massive doughnut chunks scattered around us. "Lucky," she said. "We would have been smashed flatter than pancakes."

"I know it's a Sugar Castle Competition, but a pancake is one sweet treat I do not want to be a part of," Echo said.

We all laughed, but then I saw a fin just barely peek out from the jelly oozing down the street.

"We've got to save Flash!" I cried. "He's stuck!"

Echo, Ruby, and I dashed to where Flash's fin poked out of the jelly ooze. I grabbed it with my hoof. "You two grab my tail. On the count of three, we all pull. Ready?"

Ruby and Echo got into position and nodded.

"One," I counted. "Two. Three!"

We all pulled together. We huffed and puffed and tugged. Slowly but surely, Flash's fin fully popped out of the jelly.

"It's working!" I said. "Keep pulling!"

We pulled and pulled and pulled. I could see Flash get closer and closer to the top until—

GASP!

Flash's head pulled free. He sucked in big breaths. After taking four big **gill-fuls** of water, he said, "Can you believe I could hold my breath that long? That's got to be some kind of record, don't you think? Maybe they'll put me down in the *Atlantis Book of World Records!*"

"Sounds like you're back to normal!" Echo said with a giggle.

"But still covered in jelly from the

tail down," Ruby said. "We've got a bit more work to do."

With a few more tugs, Flash was finally out.

"**The Fin-Tastic Four** could be a rescue team!" Flash said. "But maybe

we leave the GR☺W Shell out of it. It seems to cause a lot of trouble, don't you think?"

"Speaking of which," I said, "where is the GR☺W Shell?"

Echo let loose a few magic echolocation clicks. She turned around and pointed to the pile of big smashed doughnut pieces.

"My echolocation shows it in there," Echo said. "Or some of it is at least."

I swam closer. Sure enough, broken pieces of the GR☺W Shell were everywhere. It must have been smashed by the huge doughnut boulder when it fell. The shell bits didn't glow that gross orange color anymore. And now that I had a **minnow** to think, nothing was growing bigger anymore either. Not the jelly, not the Sugar Castle, not Nelia.

"I think when the GR⊛W Shell was smashed, its magic was destroyed,"

I said. I turned to my friends. "The coast is clear."

Then I looked back to the square. "Well, it isn't *clear* exactly," I said. "We have a lot of cleaning up to do."

DOUGHNUT WORRY

The huge Sugar Castles crowded everything. There were giant crab cutout cookies all over the place, sea dragon ice frosting had frozen the fountain, and the mermaid band was stuck behind a sea sponge cake tentacle.

But now that the castles weren't growing anymore, creatures were able to come out safely. Our parents led the way and rushed right over to us.

"I'm so glad you're all okay," Mom said.

"But **how in the ocean** are we going to clean up this mess?" Ruby asked.

"We could eat it!" Flash said. He took a big bite out of a lemon square the size of a door. Even though the bite was big, it only took a tiny dent out of the treat. "Eating all this might take a while."

Flash was right. Even if **every-fishy** in Mermicorn Island tried to eat

the mess, we would still be there until next year's Sugar Castle Competition.

"I don't want to burst your **BUBBLE**, Flash, but I don't think we can eat our way out of this," I said.

Talking about bubbles made me think

of the magic orange ones that came from my GR⊛W Shell. I caused this whole mess. Guilt guppies swam in my belly.

I needed to think of a way to clean everything up. I swam back and forth thinking of ways to clear the square. But I wasn't watching where I was going and smacked right into a massive doughnut.

Wait a minnow.

"That's it!" I said. "Doughnuts! I'll be right back!"

I swam up to Nelia. She was still floating over the square in her magically massive body.

"Nelia," I said. "Do you think you could use your TWISTY-TURNY SPARKLE on all the giant baked goods down below?"

Nelia nodded, and I had to dodge her big tusk. "Absolutely. Now that the GROW SPARKLE is under control, I think I can help!"

"Perfect! What if you twisted all this dough into doughnuts and wrapped them around your tusk? Then the square would be clear again!"

"My tusk would be like a doughnut kebab!" Nelia said. "I'll have this cleaned up in no time. **DOUGHNUT WORRY about a thing.**"

Nelia took a deep breath, then began to hum. I swam back down to the square, and **every-fishy** went quiet. Nelia's humming was even prettier than whale song.

As Nelia's music got louder, her tusk started to glow with **sea-utiful** yellow light. It shined so bright, I bet seagulls could even see it from the surface.

The tarts and cookies and cakes all around us started to shake.

"Is that supposed to happen?" Echo yelled up to Nelia.

Nelia didn't say anything. She just

kept humming. But she slowly nodded her
head.

The shaking got stronger and
stronger. Flash grabbed me and Ruby
and Echo into a big hug.

"It's going to be okay," I said. Nelia's
humming got louder and louder, but it was

really calming. "I feel it in my scales."

All at once, the baked goods twisted and turned and broke off into three perfectly round, giant doughnuts. There was one for each of the magnified Sugar Castles. Our kraken even looked like it was hugging itself with its big tentacles until it twirled into a doughnut shape.

As each new doughnut formed, Nelia dipped her head and looped it around her tusk.

In no time at all, the whole square was clear, and Nelia's giant tusk was covered by three huge doughnuts.

"Nelia, you did it!" I cheered.

"No, *we* did it," Nelia said. "That was a great idea about the doughnuts, Lucky. But...what do I do with all these?" She jiggled her tusk, and the big doughnuts bounced.

Baxter Beluga pulled out his **shell phone**. "I think I know **some-fishies** who can help."

10

GIGANTIC JUDGES

Nelia was still as giant as ever, but she wasn't the only big critter above the square anymore. Three huge blue whales floated with her over the Beluga Bakery.

"**Every-fishy**, I'd like to introduce you to my cousins," Baxter Beluga said. "Please welcome the Blue sisters: Violet, Mauve, and Lavender."

"Our last name might be Blue, but purple is our favorite color," Violet said.

"And doughnuts are our favorite dessert," Mauve added.

"So we're happy to help clean up," Lavender declared. "Although it looks like you've already handled that on your own."

Lavender was right. After Nelia used her TWISTY-TURNY MAGIC to clear up all the baked goods, the rest of us got to work. Mom used her BUILDER SPARKLE to rebuild Express Your Shell. The mermaids set their stage back up, and Mer-made for Music sang their latest hits. And the selkies used their **Shape-Shifting Sparkle** to turn all the jelly into *actual* jelly jellyfish.

The jelly jellyfish were **fin-credible**. They swam in silly circles, and they tasted **mer-mazing**. Fishies placed orders for them on the spot, and the selkies said there were no hard feelings that their Sugar Castle had been ruined.

"Oooh, look!" Ruby said when all the jelly cleared. She reached down and grabbed the toy trident. "The trident didn't get smashed with the **GROW Shell**. That's lucky, isn't it?"

Flash pointed at me. "No, that's Lucky!" he said. "Get it? Because his name is Lucky? Holy mackerel, I crack myself up sometimes. Don't you think that was funny?"

Every-fishy laughed. It was

basically a normal day in Mermicorn Island Square. Except for the giant narwhal with her tusk covered in huge doughnuts.

"I have an idea," Baxter said. "Just because our Sugar Castles are a bit more circular than usual doesn't mean we can't still have a competition. Ladies?" Baxter looked up at his blue whale cousins. "Would you like to be the judges?"

"Of course!" Violet said.

"What an honor," Mauve added.

"I'm positively famished!" Lavender declared. "When can we start?"

"How about now?" Baxter said.

Ruby wiggled like she was about to use her magic. But it turned out she was just doing a happy dance.

"We still get to be a part of the competition!" she said. "We didn't ruin everything after all. And we might still get to win a shot at studying with Baxter Beluga. My dessert theater can still happen!"

"And the best part is, those doughnuts are big enough for **every-fishy** to have a bite," Flash said. "Maybe even two bites. Or twenty!"

Echo held a flipper to her lips. "*Shhh! They're about to start.*"

Baxter swam up to Nelia and touched the doughnut at the tip of her giant tusk. The big treat was blue and had white frosting all over it. When his flipper touched the frosting, Baxter shivered.

"First up is the sea dragon Sugar Castle," Baxter said. "Whoops! I mean, Sugar Doughnut!"

Violet reached down and took the doughnut from Nelia's tusk. Then she took a huge bite.

"Creamy," Violet said. She handed the doughnut to Mauve, who took a big bite of her own.

"Vanilla-y," Mauve added, then passed the treat to Lavender. Lavender finished the doughnut in one gulp.

"It's so good, it sends shivers down my spine," Lavender declared, shaking

a bit from the sea dragons' ice magic.
"What's next?"

Baxter swam down Nelia's tusk to the
next massive doughnut. It was covered in
stars.

"Next is Luka Beluga's Wish upon a Starfish Doughnut," Baxter said.

Just like before, the Blue sisters finished the treat with three whale-sized bites.

"Magical," Violet said.

"Fantastical," Mauve added.

"It's so good, I wish we had more," Lavender declared. Then another massive Wish upon a Starfish Doughnut appeared out of nowhere.

"The Wish upon a Starfish magic really worked," I said. "Lavender wished for more, and then, *poof!* There it was!"

"Maybe they'll actually share this one," Flash said. His stomach growled. "Do you hear that? My tummy's rumbly."

Ruby squinted her eyes and wiggled her tail. Her BaKing SParKle glittered, and a parrotfish peach pie appeared in Flash's fins.

"Here you go, Flash!" Ruby said. "Maybe this will tide you over."

Echo's dorsal fin shook. She pointed up at Nelia, who only had one giant treat left on her tusk. "Here we go, **every-fishy**. The blue whales are about to eat your doughnut!"

"Time for our last entry," Baxter said. "From Ruby, Nelia, and Lucky!"

Hope bubbled up in my belly. Maybe we would still be able to win the baking competition!

11

BACK TO NARWHAL NORMAL

Violet took our doughnut in her flippers.
It was covered in huge crab designs
from the crab cutout cookies. It was
also that perfect bronze color from the
sea-salted caramel tart.

Violet took a big bite. "Caramel-y."

Mauve was next. "And salty."

Lavender took the last bite. "It's so good, I don't think I'll ever be **crabby** again," she declared. "The perfect end to a marvelous competition."

"But who wins?" I blurted.

I smashed my hooves over my mouth. I couldn't believe I yelled out like that.

"Sorry," I said. My cheeks had to be brighter than Ruby's tail. "I just got excited."

Baxter laughed. "Not to worry, Lucky. This is a very exciting moment. Please give our judges a **minnow** to vote on the winner."

We all floated there, waiting to hear who would be named the Sugar Doughnut champion. I was so anxious, but I realized I wasn't the only one who was feeling nervous. Nelia still floated above us in her giant form, and she kept looking at us like she wanted to be down with the group.

"Oh my goldfish!" I said. "We
need to shrink Nelia back. Flash, do
you think you can use your superspeed
to take me back to my place? I bet
Poseidon's treasure chest has a ShRINK
Shell in there."

Flash nodded and held out his fin. "You
bet! Grab on, Lucky!"

I grabbed Flash's fin with my hoof,
and in a blur of **BUBBLES**, we were in
my bedroom. We moved so fast that my
mane stuck way out behind me!

"Nice new do," Flash said. "Although,
it's not quite as pretty as Ruby's. You
should ask Nelia to style it."

"Maybe once we have her shrunk back to normal size," I said, then flipped open Poseidon's treasure chest. The first thing I saw on top of all the shimmery shells was a note! It said:

LUCKY,

WELL DONE AGAIN! IT TAKES TRUE STRENGTH TO FIX THE MISTAKES YOU'VE MADE. I'M PROUD OF YOU FOR THINKING TO USE NELIA'S SPARKLE TO CLEAN UP THE SUGAR CASTLE MESS. ONCE AGAIN, I'M VERY HAPPY THAT I CHOSE TO GIVE MY MAGIC SHELLS TO YOU.

YOU'VE ALSO LEARNED A VALUABLE

LESSON ABOUT THE SHELLS. IF THEY

ARE BROKEN, THE MAGIC WITHIN

THEM CAN GO WONKY. WHEN THE

GROW SHELL DROPPED, THE CRACK IN

ITS SIDE MADE THE SHELL CONTINUE

TO PRODUCE GROW MAGIC THAT YOU

COULDN'T CONTROL. ONLY WHEN THE

SHELL WAS COMPLETELY CRUSHED DID

THE MAGIC STOP.

THE LESSON HERE: TAKE EXTRA-

SPECIAL CARE OF THESE SHELLS. THAT

WAY YOU CAN AVOID ANY FURTHER

MISHAPS.

I THINK YOU'LL FIND THAT THE

SMALL SHELL NEXT TO THIS NOTE WILL
HELP NELIA. BY THE WAY, YOU HAVE
FANTASTIC TASTE IN FRIENDS. CONTINUE
TO SHARE THE MAGIC WITH THEM,
BOTH THE MAGIC IN THESE SHELLS AND
THE MAGIC THAT IS YOUR FRIENDSHIP.

MAGICALLY YOURS,

POSEIDON

Right on top of the treasure chest
pile was the tiniest shell I had ever seen.
It was shaped like a teeny seed, and it
was neon pink. I felt a pull in my hooves
that this was the shell Poseidon said
would help Nelia.

I grabbed it and put it in the toy trident. "All right, Flash. It's time to share the SHRINK MAGIC with Nelia."

Flash grabbed my hoof and said, "I'll get us there faster than you can say 'seahorse superspeed'!"

He was right. In no time, I was floating in front of Nelia.

"Don't worry, Nelia!" I said. "We'll have you back to narwhal normal right away."

"Thanks, Lucky!" she replied. "I was starting to feel left out that I couldn't be with **every-fishy** down in the square."

I waved the toy trident with the neon

pink ShRINk ShELL, and the teeniest-
tiniest little pink **BUBBLE** came out of
it. It popped right on the tip of Nelia's
tusk.

First, Nelia's tusk slinked back into
her head. Then her fin and her flippers

shrunk back to normal. It looked funny because her body was still giant! But then the rest of her popped back to normal size.

"Lucky, you did it!" Nelia cheered. She floated forward and wrapped me in a hug. Her tusk even went through my mane. Nelia might have been normal-sized again, but her tusk was still really long.

"Glad to have you back, Nelia," I said. "Sorry my GR⊛W Shell SParkle hit you."

"It was all an accident," Nelia said. **"Fin friends forever?"**

Tingles went up my tail that were a lot like the tingles I get from shell magic. "Of course!"

We swam back to the rest of the **Fin-tastic Four** down in the square. Right when we got next to them, the Blue sisters turned to the crowd.

Together, the three of them said, "It's time to announce the winner!"

AND THE WINNER IS . . .

"This was a tough decision," Violet said.

"It was a very close call," Mauve added.

"And we wish we could name you all champion," Lavender declared. "But there can be only one winner. And the winner is…"

The Blue sisters looked at one another, took a deep breath together, then shouted, "LUKA BELUGA!"

"His Wish upon a Starfish Doughnut blew us away," Violet said.

"Eating it was a magical experience," Mauve added.

"And the doughnut had us wishing for more," Lavender declared. "Literally."

My tail, horn, and mane all drooped at once. "Oh, **blobfish**," I said. "I think I screwed everything up. We probably got points taken away because of the GROW Shell mess."

Ruby grabbed my hoof. "Don't say that, Lucky. We made the choice to use GROW magic together!"

"That's right," Nelia said. "We were a team. And whether or not we win or lose, we do it as a group!"

"But now you're not going to get to study new recipes with Baxter," I said to Ruby. "What about your dessert theater?"

Ruby squinted her eyes and wiggled her tail. She used her Baking Sparkle to make perfect petite parrotfish peach pies. There was one for me, Nelia, Echo, Flash, and Ruby too.

"Don't you worry about that," Ruby said. "Even if I can't work with Baxter just yet, practice makes perfect. The more recipes I learn, the more I can make with my magic, and someday I know I'll grab Baxter's attention."

"You should give him one of these pies," Flash said, his mouth covered in crumbs. "If this doesn't make him want to bake with you, I don't know what will!"

"Speaking of Baxter," Nelia said, pointing toward him with her tusk. "Look at that trophy he's carrying!"

Baxter swam out of the Beluga Bakery holding a big gold trophy. It was in the shape of a glittery Sugar Castle. With the help of a selkie and his **Shape-Shifting Sparkle**, the trophy changed from a castle to a narwhal with doughnuts on its tusk. Then the gold on the front moved to spell out LUKA BELUGA, SUGAR DOUGHNUT CHAMPION.

Luka took the award with a big grin on his face. He deserved it. His Sugar Castle looked really **mer-mazing** before I ruined everything with the GROW Shell and it had to become a Sugar Doughnut. And the Blue sisters all said he made his baked treat taste great.

"I know you said it's okay, but I just want to say one more time that I really am sorry," I told Nelia and Ruby. "I'll do better next year."

Baxter Beluga turned to me and winked. "Actually, we have a new award this year that I think you're going to want to hear about."

BELUGA BAKERY BRAVERY

"A new award?" I said. "But I thought there was only one winner."

Baxter nodded. "That is normally the case. But this year, we had some *massive* change."

Guilt guppies swam back into my belly. If I had kept the GR⊛W SHELL at home, none of that massive change would have happened.

"Sometimes we make mistakes," Baxter said. "And they have effects bigger than we could ever imagine. But it is very brave to face those mistakes head-on and clean up the mess we make. So..."

Baxter swam back into the Beluga Bakery again. He came out with five gold medals, each in the shape of a doughnut.

"This year I'd like to present the Beluga Bakery Bravery Award, for helping save the Sugar Castle Competition when all seemed lost," Baxter said. "And the award goes to Ruby Scales, Nelia Tuskerson, Flash Finnegan, Echo Dolfina, and Lucky Bubbles!"

The crowd cheered. Ruby beamed. Nelia waved her tusk from side to side. None of us could believe we were getting an award!

Baxter put a shiny medal around Ruby's neck.

"**Oh my goldfish**, Lucky," Ruby said. "We won!"

"All of us!" Echo said, her dorsal fin shaking when Baxter gave her a medal.

Flash got his award next. "There is nothing in the whole wide ocean and nothing in all the seven seas that can stop the **FIN-TASTIC FOUR**!"

"That's not quite right," I said.

Flash's face fell. "It's not?"

"You're right that we're unstoppable," I said. "But we're not the **FIN-TASTIC FOUR**."

I turned to Nelia just as Baxter was placing her medal around her tusk.

"We're now the **Fin-Tastic Five**," I said.

Nelia blushed. "Do you mean it? Even though I have to go back home to Atlantis tomorrow?"

I nodded. "Of course! You'll always be a part of the group no matter where you are."

Nelia sped forward and wrapped me in a hug. We both laughed when her tusk got caught in my mane again. Then Ruby, Echo, and Flash joined in, and we all floated there, five best fin friends forever.

Even with the Beluga Bakery Bravery medal around my neck, I knew memories with my **fin-tastic** friends were the best award of all.

JASON JUNE is a writer who has always dreamed of being a mermaid. He regularly swims in the lake that he lives on and tells stories to the turtles on the beach. If he could have any kind of Sparkle, it would be Shape-Shifting Sparkle. When he finally gets that mermaid tail, he hopes it's covered in pink scales. You can find out more about Jason June and his books at heyjasonjune.com.

Half unicorn, half mermaid, and totally adorable!